Go to Sleep, Hoglet!

The Adventures of an Irish Hedgehog

Bex Sheridan

THE O'BRIEN PRESS
DUBLIN

One misty morning, in their cosy little nests, down by the banks of the river Boyne, all the hedgehogs were snuggling up for the **Big Winter Sleep**.

But one little hedgehog just
couldn't go to sleep.
Every time **Hoglet** closed his eyes,
he kept thinking about **Rabbit's**
Super Special Secret ...

About what happens
when all the
hedgehogs sleep.

When the winter wind
whirls on in.

4

When there is more night-time
and less bright-time.

When all the leaves
fall from their trees.
And all the colours come out to play …

That's when **Christmas** comes!

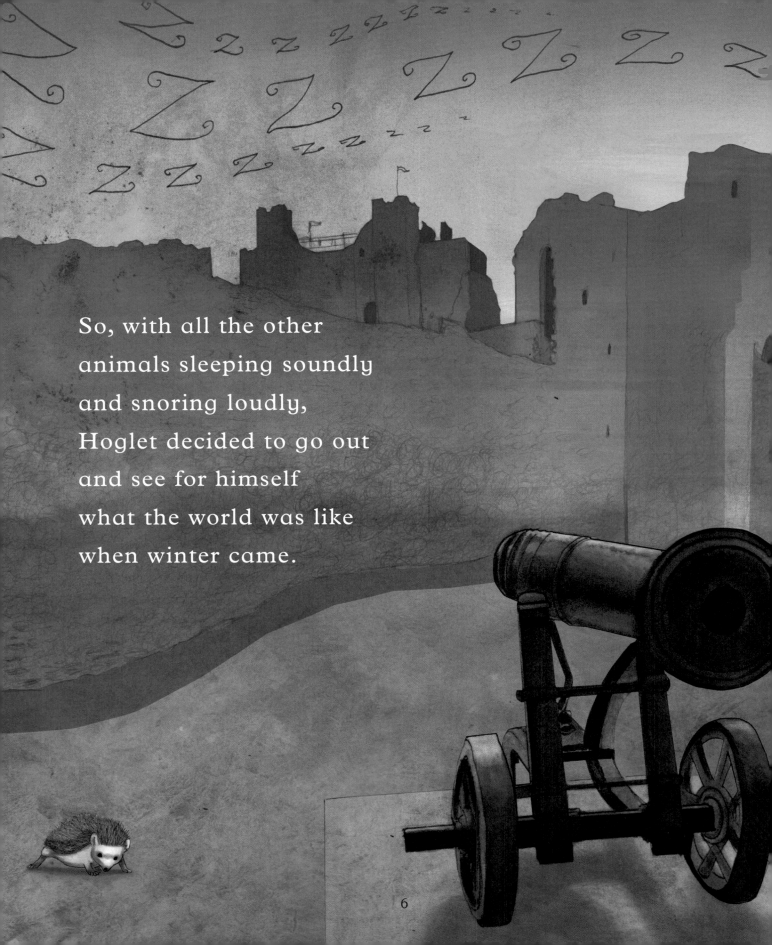

So, with all the other
animals sleeping soundly
and snoring loudly,
Hoglet decided to go out
and see for himself
what the world was like
when winter came.

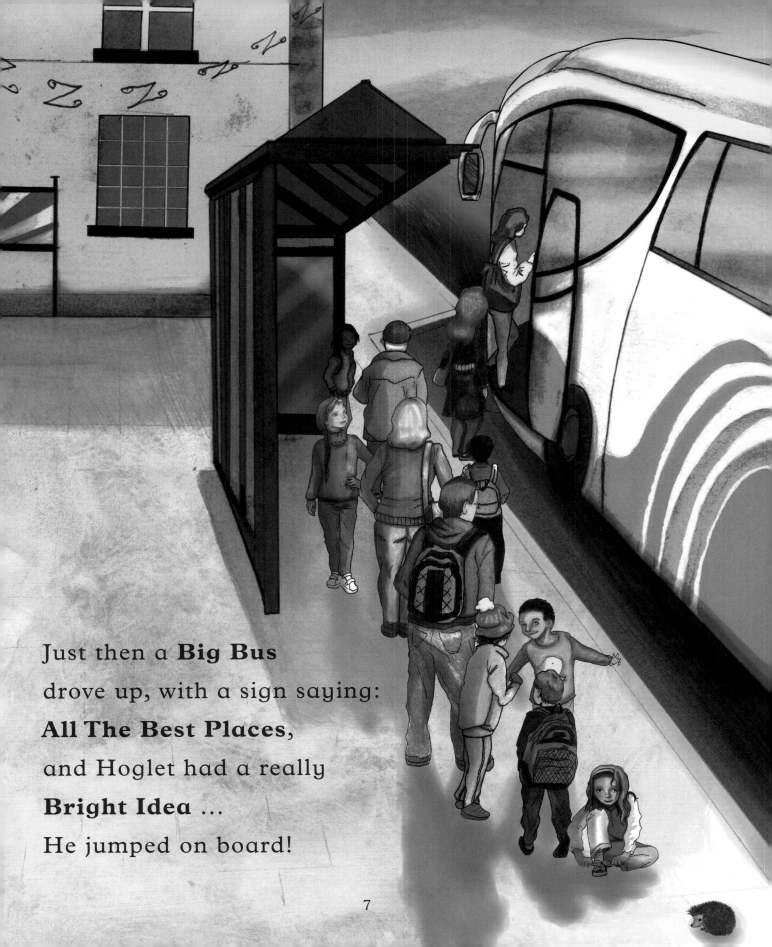

Just then a **Big Bus**
drove up, with a sign saying:
All The Best Places,
and Hoglet had a really
Bright Idea ...
He jumped on board!

7

At the very first stop
Hoglet hopped off
and met Bat.
'You'd better go
back to bed, Hoglet,'
chirped Bat.
'It's nearly time
for the **Big Scare**!'

8

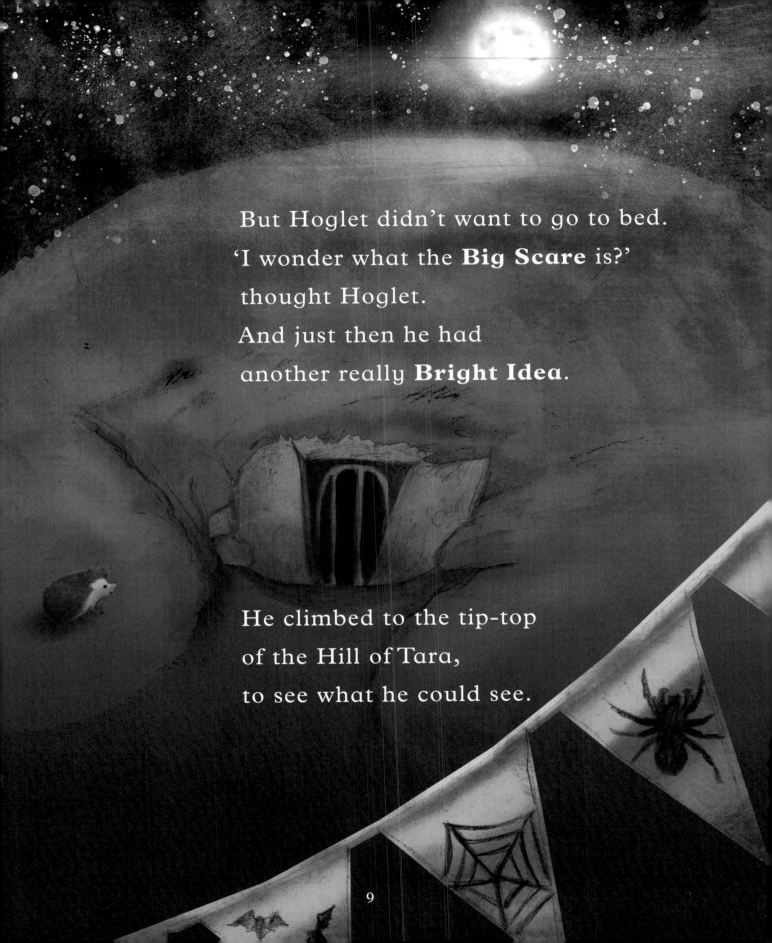

But Hoglet didn't want to go to bed.
'I wonder what the **Big Scare** is?'
thought Hoglet.
And just then he had
another really **Bright Idea**.

He climbed to the tip-top
of the Hill of Tara,
to see what he could see.

And Hoglet saw that
the **Big Scare** wasn't
so scary at all.
It was loud.
And it was colourful.
And it looked super fun.

All the small people
were just dressed as
monsters and silly things

And Hoglet said,
'If this is what autumn
is like, I can't wait
until **Christmas**!'

But Bat was still worried.
'Go to sleep, Hoglet!' Bat beeped
as he swooped away.
But Hoglet didn't want to go to sleep.
He wanted to keep on exploring.

So he started to roll back down the
Hill of Tara and that was when
Hoglet tumbled straight into **Sheep**.

'You'd better go back to bed, Hoglet,'
Sheep baahed, 'before you
catch a winter cold.'

But Hoglet didn't
want to go to bed.
So he made a wish at
Tara's Fairy Tree.
And that's when he got
yet another **Bright Idea**!
He knew just how to keep warm.

Hoglet rolled around, and
with a little help from some
lovely warm wool he was
able to heat right up.

But Sheep was still fussing.

'Go to sleep, Hoglet!' she bleated.

But Hoglet didn't want to go to sleep.

And he ran quickly on his way.

As he waited for the next
Big Bus, Hoglet started to feel
very hungry in his tummy.
And that was when sly **Fox**
snuck up ...

'You'd better go back to bed, Hoglet,' said Fox, 'or you'll get humongously hungry.'
But Hoglet didn't want to go to bed. So he thought he'd better go find some food.
And that's when he had another **Bright Idea**!

He knew just where
to find some food ...
if he could only sneak
past **Dog**.
So he waited.
And waited.
And when Dog
started chasing Fox,
Hoglet filled his tummy
with something yummy.

18

And Hoglet said,
'Now that I'm full of food,
waiting for Christmas will be easy.'
But Fox did not agree.
'Go to sleep, Hoglet!' he yipped
as he darted away.

Hoglet walked on,
wondering where he
would go next, until
he met **Badger**.

'You'd better go back to bed, Hoglet,'
yawned Badger, 'because soon
all the light will go away.'

But Hoglet didn't want to go to bed.
He had another **Bright Idea**!
'I know a **Special Sunny Place** and
on a **Special Sunny Day** the light
will be right here!'

21

As luck would have it,
the next **Big Bus** was
going that way.

But Badger did not think
that this was such a
Bright Idea.
'Go to sleep, Hoglet!'
he grumbled as the bus
trundled away.

23

When Hoglet got to **Newgrange**
and the **Special Sunny Place**,
it was already time for the
Winter Solstice and
the **Special Sunny Day**.

24

As the sun shone
into the cosy cavern,
Hoglet felt safe
and warm
and full
and not at all sleepy!
And it was almost
time for **Christmas**!

25

Hoglet squeezed his eyes shut and imagined what Christmas would be like.

He could see ...
special food,
super fun ...

26

... lots of friends and family all together.

But Hoglet wasn't with his friends or family. He was all alone.

So Hoglet had one more **Bright Idea**.
He got back on the **Big Bus**
and headed straight for Home.

Before too long,
Hoglet was right back
where he'd started from,
with all his friends and family.

Just in time for
Christmas ...
and his first
Big Winter Sleep.

31

Bex Sheridan is an artist, writer and graphic designer with a great love of animals. She is often asked to illustrate animals, from pet portraits to wildlife. Her home has its own mini-menagerie: it began with one rabbit and now there are also dogs, birds (of many kinds), a lizard and even a hedgehog – the inspiration for Hoglet! She has also illustrated and co-written *Irish Farm Animals* with Glynn Evans, also proudly published by The O'Brien Press.

Bex and pet African pygmy hedgehog, Mu.

First Published 2020 by The O'Brien Press Ltd,
12 Terenure Road East, Rathgar, Dublin 6, D06 HD27, Ireland.
Tel: +353 1 4923333; Fax:+353 1 4922777
E-mail: books@obrien.ie
Website: www.obrien.ie
The O'Brien Press is a member of Publishing Ireland.

ISBN: 978-1-78849-143-3

7 6 5 4 3 2 1
23 22 21 20

Printed and bound in Drukarnia Skleniarz, Poland.
The paper used in this book is produced using pulp from managed forests.

Go to Sleep, Hoglet! receives financial assistance from the Arts Council

Published in
DUBLIN
UNESCO
City of Literature